Hello, Benny Beaver™!

Aimee Aryal

Illustrated by Cheri Nowak

www.mascotbooks.com

It was a beautiful fall day at Oregon State University. Benny Beaver was on his way to Reser Stadium for a football game.

Benny started his journey at Memorial Union. Students nearby shouted, "Hello, Benny Beaver!"

After bowling in the Union with friends,
Benny joined a family of Beaver fans
on the quad for a picnic.

The family was happy to see their favorite mascot. They cheered, "Hello, Benny Beaver!"

In front of Valley Library, Benny ran into a librarian. The librarian called, "Hello, Benny Beaver!"

Inside, Benny checked out his favorite book. The library worker whispered, "Hello, Benny Beaver!"

Benny made his way to Dixon Recreational Center. Benny Beaver ran into students on their way into the center.

Inside, Benny exercised and lifted heavy weights. Students encouraged Benny. They chanted, "Go, Benny, go!"

Benny walked past classrooms and dormitories. Outside Weatherford Hall, Benny ran into more OSU students.

Happy to see Oregon State's friendly
mascot, students hollered,
"Hello, Benny Beaver!"

Benny's next stop was the OSU Clock Tower. A group of alumni had gathered at the Tower for a class reunion.

The alumni remembered Benny from their days at OSU. The alumni called out, "Hello, again, Benny Beaver!"

Finally, Benny Beaver arrived at
Reser Stadium – home of the
Oregon State Beavers!

Oregon State fans were ready for the
football game! They roared,
"Hello, Benny Beaver!"

Benny led the Oregon State
football team from the locker room
onto the football field.

Oregon State fans cheered for their team. The football players cheered, "Hello, Benny Beaver!"

Benny watched the game from the sidelines and rooted for the home team.

An OSU player scored a touchdown and handed the ball to Benny. The player shouted, "Touchdown, Benny Beaver!"

At halftime, the Oregon State University Marching Band ran into formation and performed *Hail to Old OSU*.

Happy to see Benny in the stands,
OSU students lifted the mascot and
cried, "Hello, Benny Beaver!"

The Oregon State University Beavers
won the football game and
beat their rivals!

Benny celebrated the victory with coaches and players. Everyone cheered, "Go, Beavs!"

After the game, Benny celebrated with happy fans all over Corvallis, Oregon.

Benny's last stop was his home. He crawled into bed and fell fast asleep.

Good night, Benny Beaver!

For Anna and Maya. ~ Aimee Ayral

For Gia. ~ Cheri Nowak

For more information about our products,
please visit us online at www.mascotbooks.com.

For more information, please contact Mascot Books,
P.O. Box 220157, Chantilly, VA 20153-0157

ISBN: 1-934878-28-6

Printed in the United States.

www.mascotbooks.com

www.mascotbooks.com

Title List

Major League Baseball

Boston Red Sox	Hello, *Wally*!	Jerry Remy
Boston Red Sox	*Wally The Green Monster And His Journey Through Red Sox Nation*!	Jerry Remy
Boston Red Sox	Coast to Coast with *Wally The Green Monster*	Jerry Remy
Boston Red Sox	A Season with *Wally The Green Monster*	Jerry Remy
Colorado Rockies	Hello, *Dinger*!	Aimee Aryal
Detroit Tigers	Hello, *Paws*!	Aimee Aryal
New York Yankees	Let's Go, *Yankees*!	Yogi Berra
New York Yankees	*Yankees Town*	Aimee Aryal
New York Mets	Hello, *Mr. Met*!	Rusty Staub
New York Mets	*Mr. Met* and his Journey Through the Big Apple	Aimee Aryal
St. Louis Cardinals	Hello, *Fredbird*!	Ozzie Smith
Philadelphia Phillies	Hello, *Phillie Phanatic*!	Aimee Aryal
Chicago Cubs	Let's Go, *Cubs*!	Aimee Aryal
Chicago White Sox	Let's Go, *White Sox*!	Aimee Aryal
Cleveland Indians	Hello, *Slider*!	Bob Feller
Seattle Mariners	Hello, *Mariner Moose*!	Aimee Aryal
Washington Nationals	Hello, *Screech*!	Aimee Aryal
Milwaukee Brewers	Hello, *Bernie Brewer*!	Aimee Aryal

College

Alabama	Hello, Big Al!	Aimee Aryal
Alabama	Roll Tide!	Ken Stabler
Alabama	Big Al's Journey Through the Yellowhammer State	Aimee Aryal
Arizona	Hello, Wilbur!	Lute Olson
Arkansas	Hello, Big Red!	Aimee Aryal
Arkansas	Big Red's Journey Through the Razorback State	Aimee Aryal
Auburn	Hello, Aubie!	Aimee Aryal
Auburn	War Eagle!	Pat Dye
Auburn	Aubie's Journey Through the Yellowhammer State	Aimee Aryal
Boston College	Hello, Baldwin!	Aimee Aryal
Brigham Young	Hello, Cosmo!	LaVell Edwards
Cal - Berkeley	Hello, Oski!	Aimee Aryal
Clemson	Hello, Tiger!	Aimee Aryal
Clemson	Tiger's Journey Through the Palmetto State	Aimee Aryal
Colorado	Hello, Ralphie!	Aimee Aryal
Connecticut	Hello, Jonathan!	Aimee Aryal
Duke	Hello, Blue Devil!	Aimee Aryal
Florida	Hello, Albert!	Aimee Aryal
Florida State	Let's Go, 'Noles!	Aimee Aryal
Georgia	Hello, Hairy Dawg!	Aimee Aryal
Georgia	How 'Bout Them Dawgs!	Aimee Aryal
Georgia	Hairy Dawg's Journey Through the Peach State	Vince Dooley
Georgia Tech	Hello, Buzz!	Vince Dooley
Gonzaga	Spike, The Gonzaga Bulldog	Aimee Aryal Mike Pringle
Illinois	Let's Go, Illini!	
Indiana	Let's Go, Hoosiers!	Aimee Aryal
Iowa	Hello, Herky!	Aimee Aryal
Iowa State	Hello, Cy!	Aimee Aryal
James Madison	Hello, Duke Dog!	Amy DeLashmutt
Kansas	Hello, Big Jay!	Aimee Aryal
Kansas State	Hello, Willie!	Aimee Aryal
Kentucky	Hello, Wildcat!	Dan Walter
LSU	Hello, Mike!	Aimee Aryal
LSU	Mike's Journey Through the Bayou State	Aimee Aryal
Maryland	Hello, Testudo!	Aimee Aryal
Michigan	Let's Go, Blue!	Aimee Aryal
Michigan State	Hello, Sparty!	Aimee Aryal
Minnesota	Hello, Goldy!	Aimee Aryal
Mississippi	Hello, Colonel Rebel!	Aimee Aryal
Mississippi State	Hello, Bully!	Aimee Aryal

Pro Football

Carolina Panthers	Let's Go, Panthers!	Aimee Aryal
Chicago Bears	Let's Go, Bears!	Aimee Aryal
Dallas Cowboys	How 'Bout Them Cowboys!	Aimee Aryal
Green Bay Packers	Go, Pack, Go!	Aimee Aryal
Kansas City Chiefs	Let's Go, Chiefs!	Aimee Aryal
Minnesota Vikings	Let's Go, Vikings!	Aimee Aryal
New York Giants	Let's Go, Giants!	Aimee Aryal
New York Jets	J-E-T-S! Jets, Jets, Jets!	Aimee Aryal
New England Patriots	Let's Go, Patriots!	Aimee Aryal
Pittsburgh Steelers	Here We Go Steelers!	Aimee Aryal
Seattle Seahawks	Let's Go, Seahawks!	Aimee Aryal
Washington Redskins	Hail To The Redskins!	Aimee Aryal

Basketball

Dallas Mavericks	Let's Go, Mavs!	Mark Cuban
Boston Celtics	Let's Go, Celtics!	Aimee Aryal

Other

Kentucky Derby	White Diamond Runs For The Roses	Aimee Aryal
Marine Corps Marathon	Run, Miles, Run!	Aimee Aryal

Missouri	Hello, Truman!	Aimee Aryal
Nebraska	Hello, Herbie Husker!	Todd Donoho
North Carolina	Hello, Rameses!	Aimee Aryal
North Carolina	Rameses' Journey Through the Tar Heel State	Aimee Aryal Aimee Aryal
North Carolina St.	Hello, Mr. Wuf!	Aimee Aryal
North Carolina St.	Mr. Wuf's Journey Through North Carolina	Aimee Aryal Aimee Aryal
Notre Dame	Let's Go, Irish!	
Ohio State	Hello, Brutus!	Aimee Aryal
Ohio State	Brutus' Journey	Aimee Aryal
Oklahoma	Let's Go, Sooners!	Aimee Aryal
Oklahoma State	Hello, Pistol Pete!	Aimee Aryal
Oregon	Go Ducks!	Aimee Aryal
Oregon State	Hello, Benny the Beaver!	Aimee Aryal
Penn State	Hello, Nittany Lion!	Aimee Aryal
Penn State	We Are Penn State!	Aimee Aryal
Purdue	Hello, Purdue Pete!	Joe Paterno
Rutgers	Hello, Scarlet Knight!	Aimee Aryal
South Carolina	Hello, Cocky!	Aimee Aryal
South Carolina	Cocky's Journey Through the Palmetto State	Aimee Aryal
So. California	Hello, Tommy Trojan!	
Syracuse	Hello, Otto!	Aimee Aryal
Tennessee	Hello, Smokey!	Aimee Aryal
Tennessee	Smokey's Journey Through the Volunteer State	Aimee Aryal
Texas	Hello, Hook 'Em!	
Texas	Hook 'Em's Journey Through the Lone Star State	Aimee Aryal Aimee Aryal
Texas A & M	Howdy, Reveille!	
Texas A & M	Reveille's Journey Through the Lone Star State	Aimee Aryal Aimee Aryal
Texas Tech	Hello, Masked Rider!	
UCLA	Hello, Joe Bruin!	Aimee Aryal
Virginia	Hello, CavMan!	Aimee Aryal
Virginia Tech	Hello, Hokie Bird!	Aimee Aryal
Virginia Tech	Yea, It's Hokie Game Day!	Aimee Aryal
Virginia Tech	Hokie Bird's Journey Through Virginia	Frank Beamer Aimee Aryal
Wake Forest	Hello, Demon Deacon!	
Washington	Hello, Harry the Husky!	Aimee Aryal
Washington State	Hello, Butch!	Aimee Aryal
West Virginia	Hello, Mountaineer!	Aimee Aryal
Wisconsin	Hello, Bucky!	Aimee Aryal
Wisconsin	Bucky's Journey Through the Badger State	Aimee Aryal Aimee Aryal

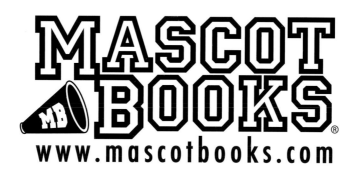
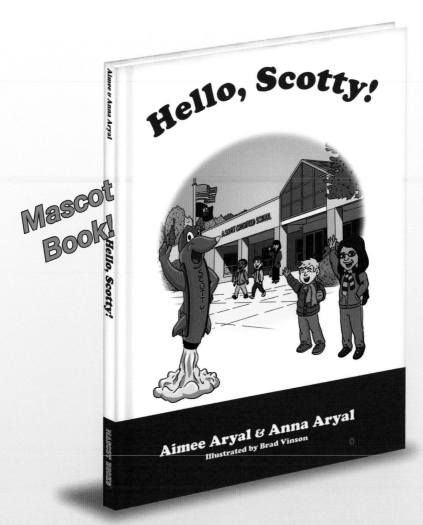

Let Mascot Books create a customized children's book for your school or team!

Here's how our fundraisers work ...

- Mascot Books creates a customized children's book with content specific to your school. When parents buy your school's book, your organization earns cash!

- When parents buy any of Mascot Books' college or professional team books, your organization earns more cash!

- We also offer options for a customized plush, apparel, and even mascot costumes!

Mascot Costumes!

Dougie the Dragon

Mascot T-Shirts!

Proud to be a Vincent Elementary Duck!

Vinny the Duck

Mascot Plush!

Lulu the Ladybug

For more information about the most innovative fundraiser on the market, contact us at info@mascotbooks.com.